MR. LEMONCELLO'S GREAT LIBRARY RACE

CHRIS GRABENSTEIN

RANDOM HOUSE 🏠 NEW YORK

Text copyright © 2017 by Chris Grabenstein
Jacket art copyright © 2017 by Gilbert Ford

Visit us on the Web! randomhousekids.com

Educators and librarians, for a variety of teaching tools, visit us at RHTeachersLibrarians.com

Library of Congress Cataloging-in-Publication Data
Names: Grabenstein, Chris, author.
Title: Mr. Lemoncello's great library race / Chris Grabenstein.
Description: First edition. | New York : Random House, [2017] |
Sequel to: Mr. Lemoncello's Library Olympics. | Summary: "Mr. Lemoncello holds a contest for his young friends where they must bring interesting facts back to his library"—Provided by publisher.
Identifiers: LCCN 2015040525 | ISBN 978-0-553-53606-5 (hardcover) | ISBN 978-0-553-53607-2 (hardcover library binding) | ISBN 978-0-553-53608-9 (ebook) | ISBN 978-1-5247-7214-7 (intl. tr. pbk.)
Subjects: | CYAC: Libraries—Fiction. | Contests—Fiction. | Books and reading—Fiction. | Eccentrics and eccentricities—Fiction.
Classification: LCC PZ7.G7487 Mm 2016 | DDC [Fic]—dc23

Printed in the United States of America
10 9 8 7 6 5 4 3 2 1
First Edition

1

This was a game Kyle Keeley refused to lose.

For the first time since Mr. Lemoncello's famous library escape contest, he was up against his old nemesis, Charles Chiltington.

"Surrender, Keeley!" Charles jeered from three spaces ahead. "Chiltingtons never lose!"

"Except, you know, when they do!" shouted Kyle's best friend, Akimi Hughes. She was ten spaces behind Kyle and couldn't stand seeing Charles in the lead.

The life-size board game had been rolled out like a plastic runner rug around the outer ring of tables in the Rotunda Reading Room of Mr. Lemoncello's library.

"The game's not over until it's over, Charles," Kyle said with a smile.

He had landed on a bright red question mark square, while Charles was safe on "Free Standing." A shaky collection of drifting holograms hovered over their heads, suspended in midair beneath the building's magnificent Wonder Dome. The dome's giant video screens were dark so they wouldn't interfere with the ghostly green images creating what Mr. Lemoncello called a Rube Goldberg contraption—a device deliberately designed to perform a very simple task in an extremely complicated way.

Most Rube Goldberg contraptions involve a chain reaction. In Mr. Lemoncello's Rickety-Trickety Fact or Fictiony game, a new piece of the chain was added every time one of the players gave an incorrect answer. If someone reached the finish line before all the pieces lined up, they won. However, if any player gave one too many wrong answers, they would trigger the chain reaction and end up trapped under a pointed dunce cap.

They would lose.

"Are you ready for your question, Mr. Keeley?" boomed Mr. Lemoncello, acting as the quiz master.

"Yes, sir," said Kyle.

"Fact or fiction for six," said Mr. Lemoncello, reading from a bright yellow game card. "At five feet four inches, George Washington was the shortest American president ever elected. Would you like to answer or do the research?"

It was a tough choice, especially since Kyle didn't know the answer.

If he did the research, he'd have to go back one space *and* lose a turn so he could look up the correct answer on one of the tablet computers built into the nearby reading desk.

But while he was researching, Charles might surge ahead. He might even make it all the way to the finish line.

On the other hand, even though Kyle didn't know the answer, if he said either "fact" *or* "fiction," he had a fifty-fifty chance of being right and moving forward six spaces, putting him *in front* of Charles, and that much closer to victory.

Of course, Kyle also had a fifty-fifty chance of being wrong and adding what might be the final hologram to the wobbly contraption overhead.

"Do the research, Kyle!" urged Akimi.

"Please do," sneered Charles.

"Yo!" shouted another one of Kyle's best buds, Miguel Fernandez. "Don't let Chiltington get under your dome, bro. He's just playing mind games with you."

"Impossible." Charles sniffed. "Keeley doesn't have a mind for me to play with."

"Uh, uh, uh," said Mr. Lemoncello. "Charles, I wonder if, just this once, you might choose kind?" He turned to Kyle. "Well, Mr. Keeley? No one can make this decision for you, unless, of course, you hire a professional decider, but trust me—they are decidedly expensive. Are you willing to put everything on a waffle and take a wild guess?"

Kyle hated losing a turn when the whole idea was to *win* the game. He hated going backward when the object was to move forward.

He studied the teetering collection of holograms suspended under the darkened dome. He looked at Charles, who was sneering back at him smugly.

"I want to answer, sir."

"Very well," said Mr. Lemoncello. "Let me repeat the question before the cucumbers I had for lunch repeat on me: At five feet four inches, George Washington was the shortest American president ever elected. Fact or fiction?"

Kyle took a deep breath. He remembered some teacher once saying people were shorter back in the olden days. So odds were that Washington was a shrimp.

"That, sir," he said, "is a . . . fact?"

A buzzer SCRONKed like a sick goose.

"Sorry," said Mr. Lemoncello. "It is, in fact, fiction. At six feet three inches, George Washington was one of our *tallest* presidents. It's time to add another piece to our dangling-dunce-cap-trap contraption."

Electronic notes diddled up a scale.

"Oh, dear," said Mr. Lemoncello. "It looks like that's the last straw!"

A hologram of a striped milk carton straw floated into place. It shot a spitball at a hologram of an old-fashioned cash register, which hit a button, which made the cash drawer pop open with a BING! The drawer smacked a holographic golf ball, which BOINKed down seven steps of a staircase one at a time until it bopped into a row of dominoes, which started to tumble in a curving line. The final domino triggered a catapult, which fired a

Ping-Pong ball, which smacked a rooster in the butt. The bird *cock-a-doodle-doo*ed, which startled a tiny man in a striped bathing suit standing on top of a fifty-foot ladder so much that he leapt off, spiraled down, and landed with a splash in a wooden bucket, which, since it was suddenly heavier, pulled a rope that struck a match, which lit a fuse, which ignited a fireworks rocket, which blasted off, which knocked the dunce cap off its hook.

The holographic hat of shame fell and covered Kyle like an upside-down ice cream cone.

"Loser!" crowed Charles.

Everybody else laughed.

By taking a wild guess, Kyle hadn't gone backward or lost a turn.

But he'd definitely lost the game!

Since the dunce cap was only a hologram, it couldn't actually trap Kyle.

But its laser-generated sides were equipped with motion sensors. So when Kyle tried to step out from under the flickering image of the giant parking-cone-shaped hat, he triggered some pretty embarrassing sound effects. Mostly gassy *BLATT*s and *FWUUUUUMP*s.

All the other players were cracking up, so Kyle took a goofy bow.

And activated the motion sensors again.

FWUUUUUMP!

"That's Keeley, all right," snickered Charles. "Nothing but windy blasts of gas."

"You're right," said Kyle, taking another bow and activating another *FWUUUUUMP!*

"And you were in the lead, Charles, so you win. Congratulations."

He stuck his hand in and out of the laser grid to blare a gassy fanfare to the tune of "Happy Birthday to You": *BLATT-BLATT-BLATT-BLATT, FWUMP-FWUMP!*

"All right," cried a no-nonsense voice in the midst of all the laughter. "Shut it down. Need to iron out that glitch."

There were six thumps and a loud whir, and then the holographic Rube Goldberg contraption disappeared. A bald man in a lab coat stepped out of the shadows, toting a tablet computer the size of a paperback.

"Switch on the Wonder Dome," he said to the flat screen he held in his palm.

Instantly, the ten wedge-shaped, high-definition video screens lining the library's colossal cathedral ceiling started shimmering as the dome went from black to its swirling, full-circle kaleidoscopic mode.

"Friends," announced Mr. Lemoncello, marching across the rotunda's marble floor toward the man in the white coat, "allow me to introduce you to the library's brand-new head imagineer, Mr. Chester 'Chet' Raymo, the genius behind my new Mind-Bogglingly Big 'n' Wacky Gymnasium Games!" He cleared his throat and warbled, *"Mr. Raymo is a brilliant brain-o! What he does is hard to explain-o!"*

Mr. Raymo was so busy tapping his tablet he didn't realize that Mr. Lemoncello was singing his praises.

The head imagineer wore thick black-rimmed glasses and a skinny black necktie and had seriously slumped shoulders. He looked like he could work at mission control for NASA.

"I believe we need to make a few minor adjustments before we roll it out to the schools," said Mr. Raymo. "Those sound effects activated when the loser attempted to escape were supposed to be burglar alarm bells, not farts."

"I know," said Mr. Lemoncello. "I changed them."

Mr. Raymo nodded. Tapped his tablet again.

"Duly noted."

"Thank you, Chet." Mr. Lemoncello threw open his arms and, in a very loud voice, addressed the players still standing in various spots along the game board.

"And thank you, one and all, for participating in this trial run of my newest gaming concept. Soon we will be able to take these same portable hologram projectors to gymnasiums, cafetoriums, and, if we hold our breath, natatoriums, so schools, even those with swimming pools, can use my life-size board games as fund-raisers—free of charge, of course."

"I really enjoyed the game," said Sierra Russell, Kyle's bookworm friend. "I was able to read two whole chapters while I waited for everybody else to spin and take their turns."

"It was awesome," agreed Kyle, who loved all of Mr. Lemoncello's wacky games, even the ones he lost.

"Totally!" added Miguel.

"It's a rip-off," scoffed Charles Chiltington, who'd been trying to run Mr. Lemoncello out of town ever since the eccentric billionaire first came home to Ohio and spent five hundred million dollars building Alexandriaville the most extraordinary high-tech library in the world.

"I beg your pardon, Charles?" said Mr. Lemoncello, blinking repeatedly. "A rip-off?"

"It's just a warmed-over version of that old parlor game Botticelli! You should be more inventive. Like the Krinkle brothers."

The Krinkle brothers owned a huge game company that, in Kyle's humble opinion, made extremely boring board games and dull generic stuff like Chinese checkers, pachisi, and dominoes. In fact, Kyle had come up with his own ad slogan for the rival game maker: "If it's a Krinkle, it's going to stinkle."

"See you later, losers." Charles marched out of the Rotunda Reading Room.

Kyle sometimes wondered why Charles was still allowed to come to the Lemoncello Library. He and his parents had done so much to try to wreck Mr. Lemoncello's dreams. Since Kyle (along with all the other "champions" from the recent Library Olympics) was now on the library's board of trustees, he once suggested that Charles (plus the rest of the Chiltington family) be banned from the building.

When he did, Mr. Lemoncello gasped, clutched his chest, and pretended that he might faint or have a heart attack. Maybe both.

"Why, if we did that, Kyle," Mr. Lemoncello had said, "we couldn't really call ourselves a library, could we?"

Kyle knew his idol was right. Libraries were supposed to be for everybody. Even jerks like Charles, who always pretended to be super polite around grown-ups—except Mr. Lemoncello.

"Not to be as nosy as Pinocchio," Mr. Lemoncello said to Sierra, "but you seemed more interested in reading your book than in marveling at my latest holographic extravaganza."

"Sorry, sir."

"Oh, there's nothing to be sorry about—a game, by the way, that I wish I had invented. I was just curious about what you were reading."

"It's called *Seabiscuit: An American Legend* by Laura Hillenbrand."

Mr. Lemoncello waggled his eyebrows, put his hand to his mouth, and hollered, "Oh, Mr. Raymo? Is there a Seabiscuit in the house?"

Suddenly, a bugle blared, a bell clanged, and two Thoroughbred racehorses, their jockeys up in the saddles, came thundering into the rotunda from the fire exit!

3

"Racing through the first turn, it's Seabiscuit leading in a surprise move!" cried the scratchy recorded voice of an old-fashioned racetrack announcer talking through his nose.

Kyle and his friends leapt out of the way as the two horses and their jockeys whipped around the rim of the rotunda as if it were a racetrack.

The breathless announcer kept going.

"Seabiscuit is in the lead by one length . . . two lengths. War Admiral is right on his heels."

Dust clouds billowed up behind the holographic horses' dirt-churning hooves.

"Down the back stretch. There goes War Admiral after him. Now the horse race is on. They're neck and neck, head and head, nose and nose. And it is either one; take your choice."

Kyle could feel the floor quaking as the two powerful horses galloped around the room.

"Go, Seabiscuit!" shouted Sierra, waving her book in the air.

"Both jockeys driving!" cried the track announcer. "It's horse against horse. Seabiscuit leads by a length. Now Seabiscuit by a length and a half. Seabiscuit by three! Seabiscuit is the winner!"

The horses vanished.

"Woo-hoo!" shouted Kyle.

"Whoa!" cried Miguel. "That was amazing!"

"That was Seabiscuit and War Admiral from their match race of 1938 at Pimlico—a racetrack near Baltimore," said Sierra.

"It was unreal," said Akimi.

"I know," said Kyle. "It was incredible!"

"No, I mean it *wasn't real*! You could see through the horses!"

"Those stupid horses scared me!" whined Andrew Peckleman, sliding his goggle-sized glasses up the bridge of his nose with one finger. "I thought they were going to run right over us. Then I realized they were just holograms!"

"Well, Andrew," said Mr. Lemoncello, "let this be a lesson to us all: The first answer isn't always the best answer. Chet?"

"Yes, sir?"

"Tell them about our brand-new Nonfictionator."

"Sorry, sir. No can do. That information is top-secret,

classified, and, I believe, restrictified. I also believe that 'restrictified' is not an actual word."

"Actually, it's a new word—one I invented and wrote down with my frindle! Plus, I hereby and forthwith—not to mention fifthwith—officially declassify and derestrictify the information in question." Mr. Lemoncello turned to the kids. "Mr. Raymo is new here at the library and somewhat shy. Perhaps, if you clap your hands as you would for Tinker Bell, we can convince him to tell us about our new Nonfictionator!"

Everybody clapped. Kyle even whistled.

"Very well." Mr. Raymo stood up and smoothed out his lab coat. "Thanks to its high-speed processor and enormous database, the Nonfictionator can generate historical holograms capable of conversing with our library patrons. Ask a question, they'll answer it. The Nonfictionator can bring historical characters to interactive life."

"With this new invention," added Mr. Lemoncello, "nonfiction doesn't have to be dry and dusty, unless, of course, it's a horse race or Lawrence of Arabia. Chet, if you please—astound me!"

"Yes, sir," said Mr. Raymo. He tapped the glass on his tablet computer.

"Careful, dear," trilled a voice from the second floor. "I smell horse poop."

"I am very familiar with horse droppings," said another.

"That's Eleanor Roosevelt," said Akimi, grabbing Kyle's arm. "She's my hero!"

"And Sacagawea!" added Miguel. "The Shoshone interpreter and guide from the Lewis and Clark expedition!"

The two holographic women descended a spiral staircase from the second floor.

"Go ahead," said Mr. Lemoncello. "Ask them a question."

Kyle couldn't resist. "Um, Ms. Sacagawea, how come you know so much about horse poop?"

"Because I know much about horses," she replied. "In 1805, when I was the only woman traveling with Lewis and Clark, they needed fresh horses to cross the Rockies. I helped them barter a pony deal with the nearest Shoshone tribe, whose leader turned out to be my long-lost brother, Cameahwait."

"Fascinating," said Eleanor Roosevelt. "We could've used your negotiating skills when creating the United Nations."

The two women drifted across the library floor toward one of the meeting rooms and then vanished.

"Now, *that's* incredible," said Andrew.

Kyle snapped his fingers. "With the Nonfictionator, we could create all sorts of new exhibits where historical holograms answer questions people ask them!"

Mr. Lemoncello slapped himself in the forehead. "Why didn't I think of that? Oh, wait. I did. Several months ago."

"Is this why we're having that special board of trustees meeting this weekend?" asked Andrew. "To unveil your new invention?"

"Perhaps," said Mr. Lemoncello mischievously. "I also have a very special announcement to make. Something that will definitely keep several board members from being bored! Oh—slight change of plans. Instead of meeting here at the library, we will gather at my new home!"

He handed out flashy business cards with an address printed on them.

"You have a new house?" asked Miguel.

"Well, it's new to me! Moved in on Tuesday. I would've moved in sooner, but it took them longer than anticipated to install the floor in the living room."

"Why'd it take so long?" asked Akimi.

"Because," said Mr. Lemoncello, "it's a trampoline."

Okay, thought Kyle. Witnessing a famous horse race and chatting with historical characters was cool. But a trampoline floor?

That was going to be awesome!

In Kansas City, Missouri, the game-making Krinkle brothers were facing a crisis.

Their newest game was a bomb. Children hated it. Parents hated it. Sales were plummeting.

In damage-control mode, the Krinkle brothers quickly convened a focus group to find out why the new product launch had been such a failure.

The two brothers, Frederick and David, who were both well over sixty, sat in a viewing room behind a one-way mirror. Both wore suits, ties, and crisp white shirts. Both fiddled with their golden "K" cuff links.

The "respondents"—children ages ten through fifteen—and a research moderator were on the other side of the glass, seated around a long conference table.

"So are you guys ready to help us make a good game even better?" asked the chipper moderator.

The children shrugged.

"I guess," said one, whose name tag labeled him as Jack. "I mean, you guys are paying us and all."

"Good attitude!" said the moderator. "Okay, you've all had a chance to play with Whoop Dee Doodle Thirteen. Reactions? Thoughts?"

The children shrugged again.

"It's sort of boring?" said a girl named Lilly.

The other kids started nodding. " 'Boring' is a good word for it," said one.

"Stupid," said a boy.

"And sad," said a girl. "It's just sad."

"It's the exact same game as Whoop Dee Doodle Twelve," added Jack. "And Whoop Dee Doodle Eleven."

In the viewing room, David Krinkle's left eye started twitching.

"That's not true," he muttered. "We put a smiley face on the whoopee cushion!"

"Ungrateful brats," mumbled Frederick, who was always a little grumpier than David.

The object of all the Krinkle brothers' Whoop Dee Doodle games was to get your teammates to guess a phrase or famous saying by using only pictures, no words. If the time in the sandglass ran out before your team guessed correctly, you had to sit on a whoopee cushion.

Whoop Dee Doodle 13 was the thirteenth edition of the game. A bright yellow starburst on the box top said it was "All New and All Fun!" The company's lawyers assured the Krinkles they could legally make that claim because the clue cards and phrases were new. So was the sandglass. It used to be pink. Now it was purple.

But customers weren't buying the claim or the game.

And it was the only new product the Krinkle brothers had in the pipeline for the coming holiday season—just six months away.

"My grandmother made me play Whoop Dee Doodle Thirteen when I was home sick from school last month," said Lilly. "It was about as much fun as the stale saltines and flat ginger ale she gave me."

"Okay, okay," said the moderator. "I'm hearing you. Let me topline these notions." He turned his back to the kids and started filling a whiteboard with words like "boring," "stupid," "sad," and "stomach flu."

While the moderator wasn't paying attention, Jack showed Lilly his smartphone.

"Have you played Mr. Lemoncello's Oh, Gee, Emoji! yet?" he whispered to her.

"No."

"Okay, let's put the phone away, Jack," said the moderator.

Jack didn't listen. "Guess the book or movie."

He showed everybody the emoji clue.

Lilly studied the phone.

The other boys and girls leaned across the table to peer at Jack's phone and try to solve the puzzle first.

 OHMY

"Got it!" said Lilly. "It's *The Wizard of Oz*!"

"Is that game fun?" asked a boy.

"Fun?" said Jack, happily imitating the tagline on every Lemoncello TV commercial. "Hello? It's a Lemoncello!"

"Enough," fumed Frederick behind the one-way mirror. "Turn them off! I hate those stupid commercials!"

David flicked the intercom switch so they wouldn't have to listen to the little monsters in the other room.

"Thirteen was bad luck," said David, his eye spasming. "That's all."

"Bad luck? It could ruin us!" Frederick was seething.

"We just need a new idea," said David. "A new game. Something spectacular. A home run!"

"We also need a way to stop Luigi Lemoncello once and for all," said Frederick, working his hands together.

"That ludicrous lunatic has been a boil on our backsides long enough."

David smirked. "The answer is simple."

"Oh, really? And how do you propose we create a new smash hit while simultaneously crushing Mr. Lemoncello's Imagination Factory?"

"Easy. We just need to increase our research and re-positioning efforts."

Frederick actually smiled. "Hmm. Too bad Benjamin Bean is no longer in our employ. He was one of the best researchers we ever hired."

"Don't worry," said David. "Our new recruit is already on the job."

"Is he up to the task?"

"Oh, yes. In fact, *she* will start this weekend!"

5

Friday night, Kyle's mother drove him to Mr. Lemoncello's home for the trustees meeting.

"I bet his house is amazing inside," said Kyle.

After the Library Olympics ended, Mr. Lemoncello had converted the main building of the Blue Jay Extended Stay Lodge, which had been Olympia Village, into a fully renovated mansion (adding a forty-foot-tall glass ceiling over the whole thing so he could see the stars at night). He kept the motel's outlying guest chalets so out-of-town trustees and their parents would always have a nice place to stay when they came to Alexandriaville for official meetings and events.

The first thing Kyle noticed when his mom pulled in was the clusters of sandbagged balloons lining the driveway.

"Balloons!" said Kyle. "I hoped there'd be balloons."

The next thing he noticed was the line of parked bookmobiles.

"I guess they picked up the out-of-towners at the airport," said Kyle.

Kyle and his mom hurried to the front door, where instead of a doorbell or knocker there was a shiny brass plaque engraved with these words: "To enter, look in the mirror and say 'emases nepo.'"

"The plaque must be the mirror," said Kyle's mom, because it was shiny enough for her to see her reflection in it.

"Emases nepo!" she said loudly.

Nothing happened.

"Wait a second," said Kyle. "It's a puzzle. If you flip the letters, like a *mirror* would, and read them backward, it says 'open sesame'!"

The instant Kyle spoke the words, the doorknob twisted and the door glided open.

Mr. Lemoncello stood on the other side.

"Welcome!" he said. He was dressed like a daredevil in bright yellow socks, a yellow flight suit, and a lemon-spangled crash helmet. "Be careful crossing the carpet in the living room, Mrs. Keeley. It's a little springy."

"I know. Kyle told me."

"Did he tell you about the bathroom?"

"No."

"It's a bouncy house. Makes using it that much more fun! So be sure to hang on to your toilet paper!"

Kyle and his mom made their way into the living room and bounded across the carpet.

"Hey, everybody—look at me!" cried Angus Harper, a kid from Texas, who'd been on the Southwest team in the Olympics. He was bouncing off the trampoline floor and leaping for the ceiling so he could try to grab one of the pairs of banana shoes dangling off the upside-down flamingo chandelier.

"Excuse me, I need something in the kitchen," said Mr. Lemoncello, sliding his feet into a pair of fuzzy slippers, which were fashioned after the fluffy frazzled birds from his video game sensation Rampaging Robin Rage.

He clicked his heels together three times and said, "To the kitchen, please!"

Four pairs of propellers twirled at the tips and heels of the slippers. Five seconds later Mr. Lemoncello rose off the floor and drifted across the room. He ducked his head under a doorjamb and disappeared.

"I have to see his kitchen!" exclaimed Kyle's mom.

"I have to have those drone slippers!" said Kyle.

They both hurried as best they could across the wobbly living room floor and into the kitchen, where they saw Mr. Lemoncello float up to retrieve a punch bowl from the highest shelf in the thirty-foot-tall pantry.

"It's just like the hover ladders in the library," said Kyle's mom.

"Except drone slippers are even better!" said Kyle.

"I want a pair," said Miguel, who was already in the

kitchen with his dad, both of them gawking at all the food being prepared by a team of chefs.

The kitchen's center island (which was shaped like Sicily) was piled high with pizza, hamburgers, hot dogs, french fries, chicken fingers, macaroni and cheese, and Hot Pockets. There was also a vegetable platter, plus a hollowed-out watermelon filled with all sorts of fruit nibbles.

Mr. Lemoncello led the team of chefs and servers into the dining room, where the legs of the massive banquet table were carved to look like the legs on a Dr. Seuss creature. Kyle's mom sat at the separate grown-ups' table (it was shorter than the one for the board of trustees). Kyle found a seat next to a girl he vaguely remembered from the Olympics. Katherine Something.

"I'm Kyle Keeley," he said, extending his hand. "I live here in Ohio."

The girl shook his hand and smiled. "I'm Katherine Kelly. From Kansas City, Missouri."

"Funny," said Kyle. "Our last names are kind of similar—so we have the same initials: KK!"

The girl laughed. "Yeah. We have something else in common, too."

"What?"

"Famous game makers live in our hometowns. You have Mr. Lemoncello; I have the Krinkle brothers!"

6

"Dinner was delicious, wouldn't you agree?" said Mr. Lemoncello, standing at the head of the very long table.

The forty or fifty kids and parents in the dining room applauded. The chefs and serving staff took a bow.

"All right," said Mr. Lemoncello. "Parents and guardians? Our security guards, Clarence and Clement, will escort you next door to the Retro Arcade, where you may play Space Invaders, Pac-Man, Donkey Kong, and all the games of your youth for free in a game center that looks—and, more important, *smells*—exactly like the mall arcades you grew up in!"

"Yee-haw!" hollered Angus Harper's father as he led the stampede of adults out of the dining room.

After they were gone, Mr. Lemoncello addressed his young trustees.

"I hereby declare this meeting of the Lemoncello

Library board of trustees officially open. I also do declare," he added in a genteel Southern accent, "that I *loved* that lemon chiffon pie! Now then, as you may have noticed, Julie of the Wolves isn't here tonight, and neither is Dr. Zinchenko. Julie is on a shelf at the library and Dr. Z is in Domodedovo, Russia, where she is celebrating her mother's birthday with pickled fish, fried cabbage dumplings, and birthday pie."

Kyle looked around the table. His friends from school—Akimi, Sierra, Miguel, and Andrew—were there, of course. But not all the members of the board of trustees could fly to Ohio for every meeting. It looked like maybe twenty other Library Olympians had made the trip, including Abia Sulayman, a very serious girl wearing a hijab, who never thought Kyle was all that funny. He also saw Diane Capriola from Georgia, Stephanie Youngerman from Idaho, and Pranav Pillai from California.

Kyle looked back to Mr. Lemoncello. He couldn't wait to hear the big announcement. He hoped it was a new game. Something as exciting as the Olympics or the escape game!

"Marjory Muldauer sends her regrets," Mr. Lemoncello said, making Kyle wait *even longer* to hear the big announcement. "Apparently, they needed her help organizing the magazine racks at the Library of Congress. Speaking of tidying things up, I would like to personally commend local board members Miguel Fernandez and

Andrew Peckleman, who earlier this week helped us with some archival items in the library's basement."

More applause.

"What'd you guys organize down there?" Kyle asked Miguel, who was sitting next to him.

"Just some papers and junk from the early days of Mr. Lemoncello's business career," said Miguel.

"And now for the first item on my agenda and also in my hands." Mr. Lemoncello held up what looked like a shiny black shoebox. A cluster of stubby antennas and strobing LEDs were arrayed along the top. Several gyrating satellite dishes the size of quarters rotated on the sides.

"For those of you joining us from out of town who did not witness last week's stunning demonstration at the library, I wanted to quickly introduce you to our newest funification device: the Nonfictionator! Chet? Tell them how it works!"

Mr. Raymo, the newly appointed chief imagineer, stood up.

"The box Mr. Lemoncello is currently holding in his hands is, of course, a portable, less powerful unit than the Nonfictionator at the library, which is supported by a massive network of mainframe computers."

"The box also operates as a universal remote!" said Mr. Lemoncello, tapping a red button on its side. The lights dimmed. He thumbed a scroll wheel. Violin music wafted out of the ceiling speakers. He scrolled again and somewhere a popcorn popper started popping. "It can control every electronic device in the house!"

"Simple infrared technology, actually," said Mr. Raymo modestly.

"And now," said Mr. Lemoncello, "I will use the device to dial up a holographic, interactive, and very attractive Supreme Court justice—Oliver Wendell Holmes Junior. He will administer our official Lemoncello Vow of Secrecy Oath before revealing something we need to keep secret."

"Holmes was on the court from 1902 to 1932," whispered Miguel.

"His opinions are still quoted and cited to this day," added Katherine Kelly from across the table.

"Oyez, oyez, oyez," said Mr. Lemoncello, bopping a button. "Here comes the judge."

The ghostly image of a very somber-looking man draped in black robes appeared next to Mr. Lemoncello at the head of the table. He sported a bushy walrus mustache and wore a starched shirt with a stiff collar that stood straight up.

"Now, if it please the court," Mr. Lemoncello said to the hologram, "will you kindly administer our super-duper double-pinky secrecy oath?"

Justice Holmes turned to the diners gathered around the table. "Please rise, raise your right hand, and repeat after me."

All the guests stood.

"I, insert your name."

Everybody said "I" and added their names.

Except Mr. Lemoncello.

He said, "I, insert your name."

The former Supreme Court justice cleared his throat disapprovingly)

"Oh. Right. I, Luigi Libretto Lemoncello . . ."

Justice Holmes continued: "Do solemnly swear or affirm that I will never reveal any of the secrets I am privy to as a member of this esteemed board of trustees. Cross my heart and hope to die, stick a booger in my eye."

When all the trustees quit giggling, they repeated the oath.

Mr. Lemoncello flicked off the Nonfictionator. Justice Holmes disappeared.

"Since you are all duly and officially sworn to secrecy," said Mr. Lemoncello, "how'd you like a sneak peek at what I hope will be my game company's biggest hit this holiday season?"

"Woo-hoo!" shouted Kyle.

"We'd love it!" added Angus.

"Very well," said Mr. Lemoncello. "But remember—it's a secret. Even Santa doesn't know about it yet!"

7

"Right now," said Mr. Lemoncello, "the tremendous holographic magic of the Nonfictionator only works inside the library or here in this extremely expensive portable unit. But . . ."

Mr. Lemoncello let everybody hang in suspense for a few seconds.

Finally, when Kyle thought he might burst, Mr. Lemoncello tapped the remote button on top of the Nonfictionator box.

A giant flat-screen TV brightened inside the wall behind him.

"This November," he announced, "just in time for the holiday shopping season, we will introduce what could be a real game changer of a game. Fantabulous Floating Emoji! It's like charades, except the clues are given by three-D emoticons projected over the board by the 'magic holographic eye'!"

A computer-generated animation of the game appeared on the TV screen. There was a trail of spaces winding around the edges of the board. An emerald-green disk sat in the center, between stacks of red, green, blue, and yellow cards.

"Choose a category!" said Mr. Lemoncello.

On the screen, an animated yellow card flipped over to reveal "classic children's books."

Suddenly, a three-dimensional rotating plate of spaghetti—complete with a twirling fork—floated over the board.

"That is so cool!" said Pranav.

"*Cloudy with a Chance of Meatballs*!" guessed Andrew.

Mr. Lemoncello honked like a goose. "Sorry. Incorrect. Next emoji!"

A rotating apple appeared next to the spaghetti.

"Johnny Appleseed's Italian grandmother!" guessed Akimi.

Everybody sort of looked at her.

Mr. Lemoncello goose-honked again.

A third emoji appeared over the board: a fuzzy bug.

"Finding the Worm by Mark Goldblatt?" said Sierra hesitantly.

This time Mr. Lemoncello just shook his head.

A fourth and fifth 3-D emoji simultaneously materialized over the game board: a hamburger and a lollipop.

"The Very Hungry Caterpillar!" shouted Kyle.

"Ding, ding, ding!" said Mr. Lemoncello. "We have a winner!"

"Yes!" Kyle arm-pumped in triumph.

"Way to go, bro," said Miguel.

Mr. Lemoncello bopped a button on his boxy controller, and the screen went blank.

"We are all set to begin production next week so that this holiday season kids everywhere can bring home their own hologram projector at a reasonable price. It's so cheap even my family could've afforded it. And we were so poor we used to eat cereal with a fork to save money on milk!"

Everyone laughed.

"Thank you," said Mr. Lemoncello. "I'm here all week." He brandished a rolled-up tube of blueprints. "And these are the incredibletastic new game's complete design schematics."

He bent down and pulled back the rug to reveal a floor safe.

"Should I not be able, for whatever reason, to fulfill my duties as head of the Imagination Factory, I want you, my trusted trustees, to pick up the torch and carry on. Not that I want you to burn these blueprints to make a torch, mind you, because you will need them to build the board game. You will also need to know the combination to this floor safe. Kindly keep it a secret, too, for it is the same series of random letters I use all the time: R right. E left. A right. D left. That's right. There's nothing left. It's just R-E-A-D. The key to unlocking everything in the universe!"

Across the table, Katherine Kelly was writing the combination down in her small notebook. Kyle didn't need to. He could memorize four letters. Heck, anybody could.

"So much for fun and games," said Mr. Lemoncello. "Let's move on to the next item on our agenda. Lemoncello Library business."

Sierra, Pranav, and Andrew clapped.

Kyle wanted to play another round of Fantabulous Floating Emoji or hear the exciting announcement Mr. Lemoncello had promised he was going to make. Library business sounded boring.

"It's time for my major announcement!" said Mr. Lemoncello.

Woo-hoo, thought Kyle. So much for being bored. It was showtime!

"To thank you all for your dedicated service," said Mr. Lemoncello, "I have created a brand-new, board-members-only board game—without a board!"

Kyle leapt out of his seat. "Yes!"

He pumped both fists over his head.

Everybody else just stared at him.

"Sorry."

Kyle sat back down.

"No need to apologize, Mr. Keeley!" exclaimed Mr. Lemoncello. "For I am as excited as you are. Now then, where was I? Ah, yes. My dining room. But this game will take you far, far away from here! And if you win, it will take you even farther—on a tour of libraries all across North America!"

Now Kyle was super excited. He and his family had never really done much traveling. Except to Disney World. Once.

Oh, they'd also been to Cedar Point, an amusement park in Ohio. Kyle tried to forget that trip. His brother Curtis had thrown up on the Corkscrew roller coaster. Kyle was in the seat in front of him.

"What's this new game called?" asked Akimi.

Before he replied, Mr. Lemoncello struck a finger-pointed-to-the-sky pose, just like his statue in the fountain in the lobby of the library—only there wasn't any water spurting out of his mouth.

"Mr. Lemoncello's Fabulous Fact-Finding Frenzy!"

Angus Harper's hand shot up.

"Yes, Angus?"

"Are you sure it's a game, sir? Finding facts sounds an awful lot like a homework assignment."

"Oh, it's a game, all right," said Mr. Lemoncello. "Perhaps the most challenging one any of you will ever play. That's why the prize is so amazerrific. And why only ten of you will even have a chance of winning it!"

8

All the trustees were buzzing excitedly.

Mr. Lemoncello tapped the side of his water glass with a spoon to regain everyone's attention.

"The Fabulous Fact-Finding Frenzy will consist of two rounds," he announced. "The first elimination round I like to call 'the elimination round,' because it is the round in which players will be eliminated. You will be paired up in two-person teams as we endeavor to see who amongst you is most like Mike Mulligan with his steam shovel and knows how to dig, dig, dig. The top five teams, consisting of ten players total, will move on to round two. The rest of you will be sent home with lovely parting gifts."

"What's the second round, sir?" asked Pranav Pillai.

"Ah! Good question, Pranav."

"Thank you, sir."

"The second round will come after the first one and last a few days, so you might need to miss some school. . . ."

"Woo-hoo!" shouted Kyle, doing a quick raise-the-roof dance move.

Everyone else stared at him. They were mostly brainiacs. Not that there was anything wrong with that. They just seemed to enjoy going to school, doing homework, and memorizing math junk more than Kyle did.

"The second round of the game," Mr. Lemoncello continued, "is the actual Fact-Finding Frenzy! In it, our top ten research assistants will race against each other to see who can solve clues, unravel puzzles, pass through roadblocks, and overcome any and all obstacles to find the fascinating fact we're looking for!"

Kyle was super excited. This new game reminded him of that TV show where contestants raced each other around the world. It was one of his faves.

"The facts," Mr. Lemoncello continued, "will be linked to the five new interactive Nonfictionator displays we're creating for the library. Displays that will be revealed to the public at a grand gala featuring cake, balloons, indoor fireworks, confetti cannons, and a surprise guest appearance by the one and only Haley Daley!"

Everybody cheered.

Haley had been one of the winners in the first escape game but had since moved out to Hollywood, where she was now a TV and singing star on the Disney Channel.

"Who are the five historical figures to be honored with new exhibits?" asked Stephanie Youngerman from Idaho.

"Those names will not be revealed until round two," said Mr. Lemoncello. "We're still tweaking the list."

Mr. Lemoncello went on to explain that the library lobby would be home base, just like the home square from his first big hit, the board game Family Frenzy, which he invented when he was still a teenager. It was the game that earned the bazillionaire his first millions.

The teams in round two would race each other—out into the field and back to the library.

"You may need to travel on planes, trains, and automobiles," said Mr. Lemoncello. "Not to worry. Our fleet of bookmobiles will be at your disposal—as will my corporate jets, airplanes, and helicopters. So be sure your parents or guardians sign these permission slips."

He handed out tightly rolled-up scrolls of paper.

"They're kind of long," muttered Andrew after opening his.

"Oh, yes," said Mr. Lemoncello. "Because they cover everything—even stuff I haven't thought of yet!"

Akimi raised her hand.

"So what does the winning team actually win?" she asked.

"Something more priceless than a million dollars, because let's face it, a million dollars has a price: one million dollars. If you win, you will tour the country with these holographic exhibits and see North America—for free!"

"Wait a second," whined Andrew Peckleman. "I thought these new exhibits were for *our* library, downtown."

"At first," said Mr. Lemoncello. "Then, in the fall, we will take the Nonfictionator and our team of fabulous fact finders on the road to libraries all over North America! Whoever wins will have an all-expenses-paid trip to see Washington, Chicago, New York, Seattle, Vancouver, and San Francisco, where you will be greeted as library rock stars! But wait, there's more. The two members of the winning team will also be the first two people in the whole entire world—including Antarctica—to take home my new Fantabulous Floating Emoji game the instant it rolls off the assembly line!"

Kyle's heart started beating a little faster.

It always did that whenever he wanted to win, win, win!

MR. LEMONCELLO'S GREAT LIBRARY RACE BOOK LIST

Here's a complete list of the books mentioned or alluded to in *Mr. Lemoncello's Great Library Race*. How many have *you* read?

☐ *The Age of Edison: Electric Light and the Invention of Modern America* by Ernest Freeberg

☐ *Alexander and the Terrible, Horrible, No Good, Very Bad Day* by Judith Viorst

☐ *Charlie and the Chocolate Factory* by Roald Dahl

☐ *Cloudy with a Chance of Meatballs* by Judi Barrett and Ron Barrett

☐ *The Crossover* by Kwame Alexander

☐ *The Ear, the Eye, and the Arm* by Nancy Farmer

☐ The Encyclopedia Brown series by Donald J. Sobol

☐ *Escape from Mr. Lemoncello's Library* by Chris Grabenstein

☐ *Everything on a Waffle* by Polly Horvath

☐ *Finding the Worm* by Mark Goldblatt

☐ *Fortunately, the Milk* by Neil Gaiman

☐ *Frindle* by Andrew Clements

☐ *The Gollywhopper Games* by Jody Feldman

☐ The Harry Potter series by J. K. Rowling

- [ ] *Hatchet* by Gary Paulsen
- [ ] *The Higher Power of Lucky* by Susan Patron
- [ ] *Horton Hatches the Egg* by Dr. Seuss
- [ ] *Julie of the Wolves* by Jean Craighead George
- [ ] *Laughing at My Nightmare* by Shane Burcaw
- [ ] *Lawrence of Arabia: The Authorized Biography of T. E. Lawrence* by Jeremy Wilson
- [ ] *The Lion, the Witch and the Wardrobe* by C. S. Lewis
- [ ] *Mike Mulligan and His Steam Shovel* by Virginia Lee Burton
- [ ] *Oh, the Places You'll Go!* by Dr. Seuss
- [ ] *Penny from Heaven* by Jennifer L. Holm
- [ ] The Percy Jackson and the Olympians series by Rick Riordan
- [ ] *Peter Pan* by J. M. Barrie
- [ ] *Pinocchio* by Carlo Collodi
- [ ] *The Puzzling World of Winston Breen* by Eric Berlin
- [ ] *Roget and His Thesaurus* by Jen Bryant
- [ ] *Seabiscuit: An American Legend* by Laura Hillenbrand
- [ ] *Timmy Failure: Mistakes Were Made* by Stephan Pastis
- [ ] *Unstoppable* by Tim Green
- [ ] *The Very Hungry Caterpillar* by Eric Carle
- [ ] *The Westing Game* by Ellen Raskin
- [ ] *Wicked: The Life and Times of the Wicked Witch of the West* by Gregory Maguire
- [ ] *Wonder* by R. J. Palacio
- [ ] *The Wonderful Wizard of Oz* by L. Frank Baum
- [ ] *A Year Down Yonder* by Richard Peck

A Q&A WITH AMERICA'S FAVORITE GAME MAKER—
CHRIS GRABENSTEIN

Tess Steinkolk

1. **How much do you relate to Mr. Lemoncello? How easily does his voice come to you while you're writing?**
   At a lot of the schools I visit, the teachers and kids call me "Mr. Lemoncello" instead of "Mr. Grabenstein" before catching themselves. I can't blame them. I am a wacky adult who hasn't forgotten how it feels to be a kid—just like Luigi Lemoncello. I tell people that Mr. Lemoncello is a mix of the improvisational comic I used to be, the late Robin Williams, and the late Jim Henson, whom I had the great good fortune to write for back in the 1980s. Jim Henson had an extraordinarily creative imagination and all the money in the world (or so it seemed to me at the time). If he wanted to do something wacky— like have an animatronic Gonzo puppet snap a flash picture of everyone who stepped through the front door of his offices—he did it. The voice for Mr. Lemoncello was hard to discover at first. But now, three books into the series, it's like playing instead of working. In fact, on days when I know I am writing a Lemoncello scene, I'm as giddy as he would be in a new pair of banana shoes.

2. **The Lemoncello books are packed so full with facts and trivia. What kind of research goes into writing this series?**
   The research is constant and daily. In my writing room, I have a laptop computer hooked up to a monitor. The manuscript in progress lives on the monitor screen; research is up on the laptop screen. Recently, I did more research by attempting my first-ever "escape room" adventure with my wife and a couple of friends. There were only four of us in a room that typically needs eight people to find and work all the clues. We almost made it out in under an hour. Almost. I also like to visit museums to see how they are making information come to life for their visitors. That's what Mr. Lemoncello is all about!

A Q&A WITH AMERICA'S FAVORITE GAME MAKER—
CHRIS GRABENSTEIN

3. **What important lesson do you want readers to take away from this series?**
The motto chiseled into Mr. Lemoncello's statue: "Knowledge not shared remains unknown." I guess that's another way of saying that we're all stronger when we work together. There is also a powerful teamwork theme running through all three books. In *Mr. Lemoncello's Great Library Race*, I was inspired by a teacher I met who told me that she wished I would write a book showing that "research means you go back and re-search. You don't just take the first answer you find on Wikipedia." I also want kids to think of research as a fun game. It will make doing all those term papers in high school and college a little easier and maybe even fun.

4. **Where do you do most of your writing?**
I do a lot of my writing in the second bedroom of our two-bedroom apartment in New York City. However, since I travel so much to visit schools, bookstores, and conferences, I am also quite adept at writing in planes, trains, and automobiles. Fortunately, I can write to music. So I create a playlist (usually made up of movie soundtracks) that fits the tone of whatever I am working on, slip on my headphones, and get lost in whatever world I am writing about that day.

5. **You've written so many different books. Do you ever run out of ideas?**
Not yet! In fact, sometimes I have too many ideas and there isn't time to write and publish them all. I think my prolific output is partially fueled by my seventeen years in advertising where we wrote from nine to five every day and created two hundred scripts that the client would kill for every one that was finally produced. But, writing has never felt like work. For me it's fun. I am very lucky that I can make a living doing what I love— playing with words and characters and spinning stories.

6. **What's the strangest thing that's ever inspired you to write a book or a piece of a book?**
Middle school lockers! That's what inspired the third book in my *Haunted Mystery Series* (the one originally titled *The Smoky Corridor* now re-released as *The Zombie Awakening*). I was visiting lots of schools to promote the first two books in that series, and I noticed the rows and rows of locked metal boxes lining the hallways. To my ghost-story-spinning brain, they looked like upright tin coffins. I wondered, "What if every one of those lockers was haunted by a ghost?" Then I had to figure out, why? Why were so many ghosts hanging out in middle school lockers? Aha! They were relatives who had passed away but came back to protect the kids going to that school. Okay, but once again, why? Because . . . uh . . . there was a zombie slumbering in the basement who had just woken up and was hungry for young brains! Yep. That's where stories come from. You start with a strange what if and see where it leads.

RACE THROUGH
MR. LEMONCELLO'S LIBRARY!

If Kyle can make it through the first round of Mr. Lemoncello's fact-finding competition, he and the other lucky finalists will go on a great race—by bicycle, bookmobile, and even Mr. Lemoncello's corporate banana jet!—to find fascinating facts about famous Americans. Can YOU make it through Mr. Lemoncello's great maze of library facts without making a wrong turn? Try your hand at the maze below as practice!

Answer on page 53

TRIVIA QUESTIONS

Find the answers in
Mr Lemoncello's Great Library Race!

1. Which president's personal library of approximately six thousand books became the basis of the Library of Congress?

2. What was the name of Thomas Edison's first movie?

3. What poet wrote the poem "I dwell in Possibility"?

4. Who was the youngest witness to the Wright brothers' first flight?

5. Which author's book features a secret passageway through a wardrobe?

6. What is the name of the character who grew up to be the Wicked Witch of the West, in Gregory Maguire's book *Wicked*?

7. How many shots has Michael Jordan missed in his basketball career?

8. Who is the author of *Hatchet*?

Answers on page 53

MR. LEMONCELLO'S GREAT LIBRARY GAME

"Sometimes you have to re-search for things you
might've missed the first time you searched."

Re-search through your library the way Kyle and his friends do in
Mr. Lemoncello's Great Library Race with this Lemoncello-style
scavenger hunt for your library!

SET UP

Review the game components provided for four teams to play:

- 1 GAME MASTER GUIDE that guides you in leading the game with either the clue cards or the pictogram cards.
- 4 CLUE CARDS (1 for each team).
  - For a less challenging game that will be more like a traditional scavenger hunt, use the 4 PUZZLE CARDS (1 for each team).
  - For a more challenging game, use the 4 PICTOGRAM CARDS (1 for each team).
- 4 ANSWER SHEETS (1 for each team).
- Hide the PICTOGRAM or PUZZLE cards in the following books or areas of your nonfiction collection. You might want to affix a temporary Do Not Remove from Shelf sticker on these books until the game is over.

000–100s	Book about or mentioning the Bermuda Triangle
200s	Book on saints
300s	Stone Soup book
400s	Book on sign language
500s	Book on planets
600s	Book on horses
700s	Garfield book
800s	A Shel Silverstein book
900s	Book on Washington, D.C.

WILD CARD *The Tale of Despereaux*

GAME PLAY

- Each team is given an envelope with CLUE CARDS in random order.
- Each team draws one CLUE CARD at a time from the envelope and sets out to find the BOOK hinted at on the card.
- Teams can use any physical library resource and catalog computers ONLY to assist them in their search.
- The first team to correctly complete the answer sheet is declared the winner!

MORE WAYS TO PLAY

- If your library has iPads or other portable devices with Internet access, send the teams to separate areas of the library. This way teams can access the library's online catalog and will not be able to hear any answers from another team.

- Instead of handing out the entire envelope with all ten CLUE CARDS, have the team return to a central table where a librarian can hand the team their next card. This will help prevent teams from all being in the same area at the same time.

GAME MASTER GUIDE

THE CLUES

000–100s—If you connect these dots, the line makes a triangle, which is commonly referred to as the Bermuda Triangle. Hide either the 000–100s Word Card or Pictogram Card inside a book in the 100s section about the Bermuda Triangle.

200s—The "elevated" Christopher, Francis, and Teresa are all saints. Hide either the 200s Word Card or Pictogram Card inside a book about the life of the saints.

300s—This recipe plus the "rock" hints should send players to the 300 section looking for a cookbook. Hide either the 300s Word Card or Pictogram Card inside a book with a recipe for Stone Soup.

400s—Want to speak volumes without making a sound? Then you need to learn sign language. Hide the 400s Word Card or Pictogram Card inside a book about sign language.

500s—"My Very Exciting Magic Jeep Slid Under Norway" is a way to memorize the order of the planets in our solar system. Hide the 500s Word Card or Pictogram Card inside a book about the planets.

600s—Mister Ed, Seabiscuit, Trigger, Misty, Black Beauty? Hide the 600s Word Card or Pictogram Card inside a book about horses.

700s—Who is the most famous lasagna lover in the world? Hide the 700s Word Card or Pictogram Card inside any Garfield book.

800s—*Where the Sidewalk Ends. Falling Up. A Light in the Attic.* Hide the 900s Word Card or Pictogram Card inside any Shel Silverstein book.

900s—Yes, it's true—the Mall in Washington, D.C., has no stores or food court. Hide the 900s Word Card or Pictogram Card inside a book about Washington, D.C.

WILD CARD—All the clue words point to one award-winning piece of fiction. Hide the Wild Card Word Card or Pictogram Card inside *The Tale of Despereaux.*

GAME MASTER GUIDE

THE PICTOGRAMS

000–100s—Half of yo-yo = YO. Add UR and you end up with: <u>YOUR</u>

200s—The universal symbol for everybody's favorite place: <u>LIBRARY</u>

300s—Remember the periodic table of elements? If not, it's probably in the 540s section of your library. Element 53 is I for iodine; 16 is S for sulphur. Put them together: <u>IS</u>

400s—This one had better be easy after that last one. It is what it is: <u>KEY</u>

500s—Another easy one. The Roman numeral for two, or: <u>TO</u>

600s—The letter O plus a PEN: <u>OPEN</u>

700s—Start with the verb POUR, then change the P to Y: <u>YOUR</u>

800s—Exactly what you see with your own eyes: <u>EYES</u>

900s—We have a TOW truck, but we take away the W and end up at: <u>TO</u>

WILD CARD—No, it's not a globe, it's the: <u>WORLD</u>

So a winning answer sheet should read . . .

<u>YOUR</u> <u>LIBRARY</u> <u>IS</u> the <u>KEY</u> <u>TO</u> <u>OPEN</u> <u>YOUR</u> <u>EYES</u> <u>TO</u> the <u>WORLD</u>.

Game created by Darrel Robertson, Children's Services Supervisor, and Melanie Fitz, Children's Library Associate, Carroll County Public Library, Finksburg, MD.

MR. LEMONCELLO'S
GREAT LIBRARY GAME
ANSWER SHEET

Team Name: _____

_____
000–100s

_____
200s

_____ the _____
300s   400s

_____   _____
500s   600s

_____   _____
700s   800s

_____ the _____.
900s   WILD CARD

THE CARDS

✂ -

000–100s
Connect the dots: 1=Miami, Florida, 2= San Juan, Puerto Rico, 3=Bermuda, and 4= Miami, Florida

200s
This title elevates Christopher, Francis, and Teresa above all others.

300s
This recipe is good with a carrot or two, some meat; many like cabbage in it . . . but you definitely need an igneous, sedimentary, or metamorphic ingredient.

400s
I speak volumes without ever making a sound.

500s
My Very Exciting Magic Jeep Slid Under Norway. This helps me keep the eight straight.

600s
Mister Ed told me once to throw a Biscuit into the Sea and that Trigger-ed me to remember a Misty Beauty-ful Black morning.

700s
Lasagna is my favorite part of every lazy day.

800s
When the sidewalk ended, I fell up and noticed a light in the attic.

900s
WHAT!!! This town's Mall has no stores?!

WILD CARD
Don't despair, a mouse, a princess, some soup, and a spool of thread are the recipe for an award-winning book.

THE PUZZLE CARDS

000–100s YOUR

200s LIBRARY

300s IS

400s KEY

500s TO

600s OPEN

700s YOUR

800s EYES

900s TO

WILD CARD WORLD

PICTOGRAMS

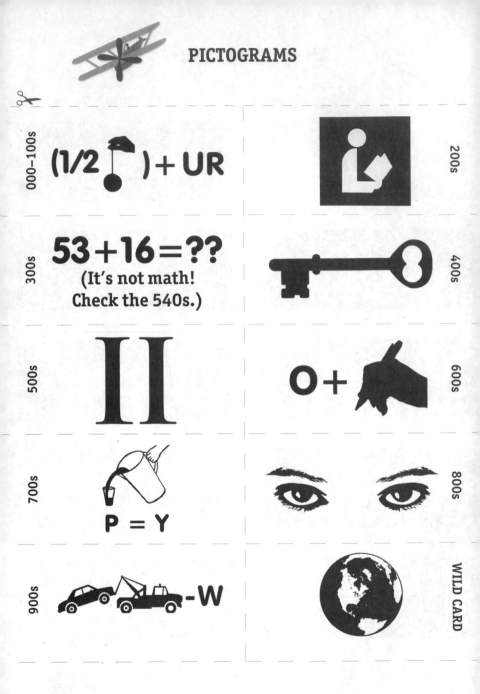

000–100s

$(1/2 \; \text{🌂}) + \text{UR}$

200s

300s

$53 + 16 = ??$
(It's not math!
Check the 540s.)

400s

500s

II

600s

$O+$

700s

$P = Y$

800s

900s

$-W$

WILD CARD

52

ANSWER KEY

Answer to Maze (page 44):

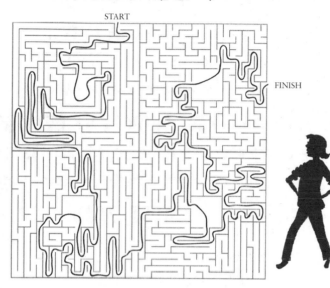

Answers to Trivia Questions (page 45):

1. Thomas Jefferson
2. *The Great Train Robbery*
3. Emily Dickinson
4. Johnny Moore
5. C. S. Lewis
6. Elphaba
7. More than nine thousand
8. Gary Paulsen